LOVELY DAY

BASED ON THE SONG BY **BILL WITHERS** AND **SKIP SCARBOROUGH**

ILLUSTRATED BY OLIVIA DUCHESS

SCHOLASTIC INC.

When I wake up in the morning, love
And the sunlight hurts my eyes . . .

And something without warning, love

Bears heavy on my mind . . .

Then I look at you
And the world's alright with me.

Just one look at you
And I know it's gonna be . . .

LOVELY DAY

A LOVELY DAY

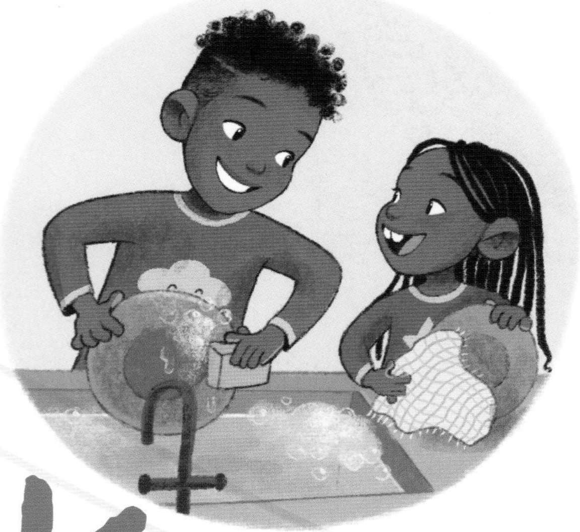

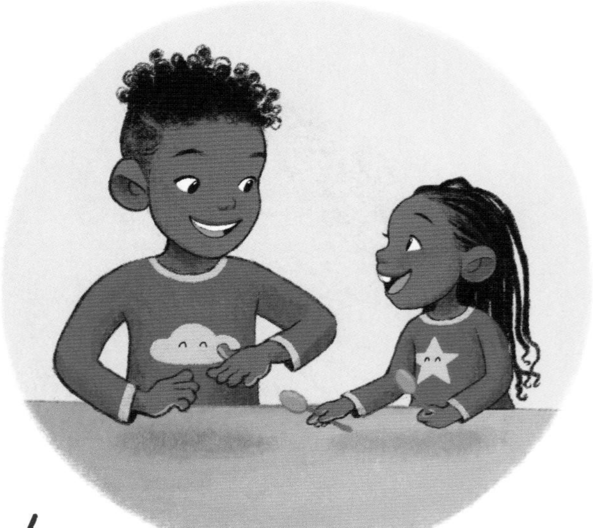

LOVELY DAY

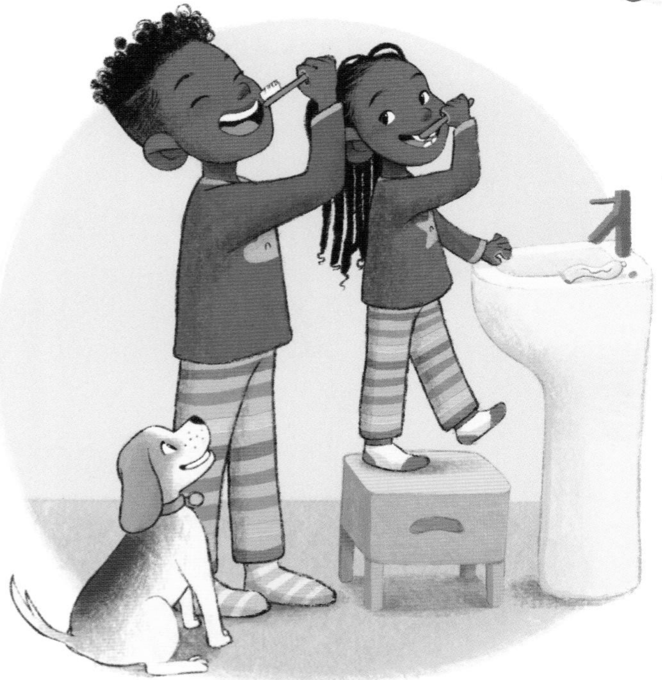

LOVELY DAY

LOVELY DAY

LOVELY DAY

LOVELY DAY

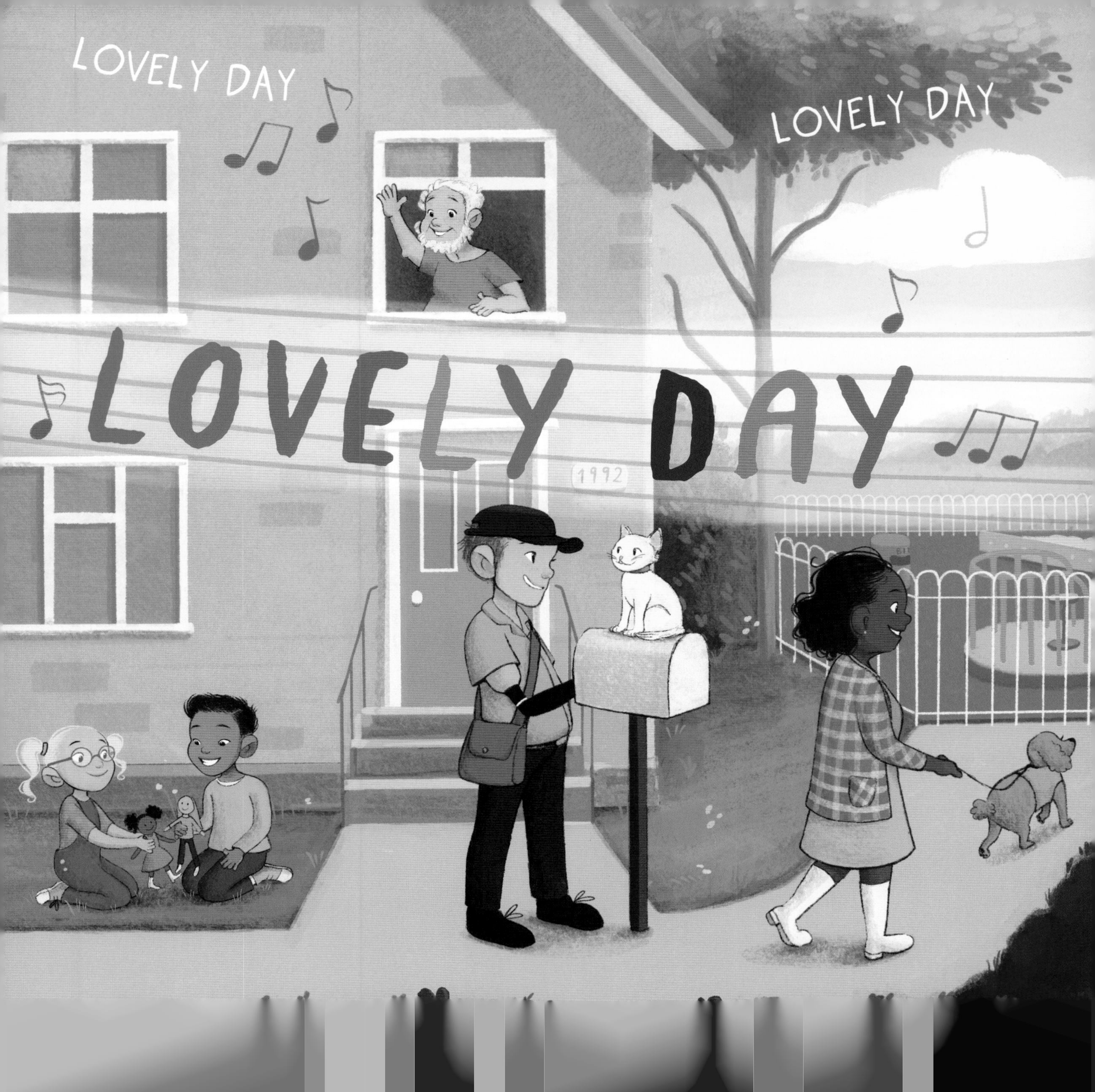
LOVELY DAY
LOVELY DAY
LOVELY DAY
1992

When the day that lies ahead of me

Seems impossible to face . . .

When someone else instead of me
Always seems to know the way . . .

Then I look at you . . .

And the world's
alright with me.

Just one look at you

And I know it's gonna be . . . .

LOVELY DAY

A LOVELY DAY!

LOVELY DAY

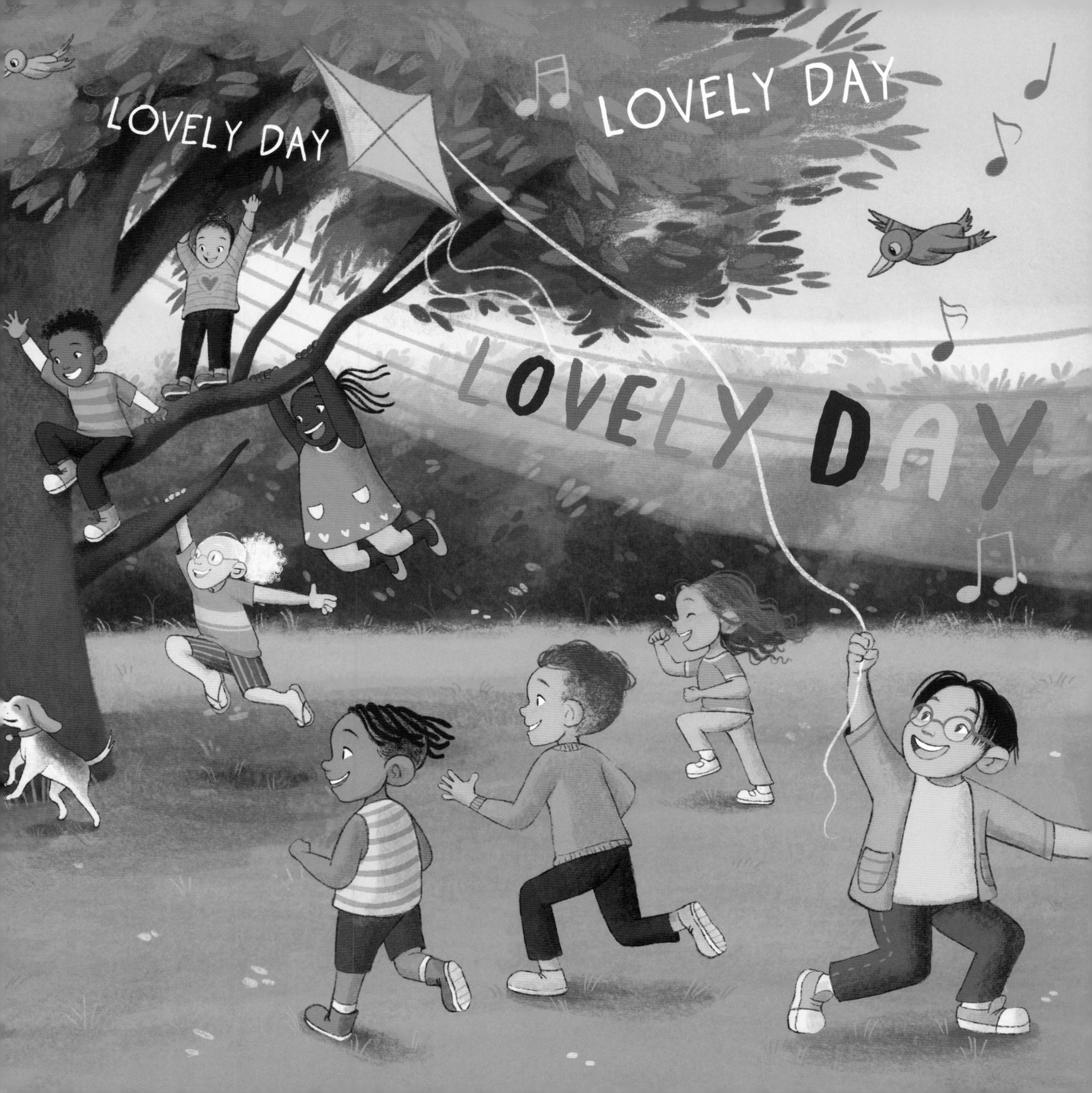
LOVELY DAY
LOVELY DAY
LOVELY DAY

A LOVELY DAY

LOVELY DAY

LOVELY DAY

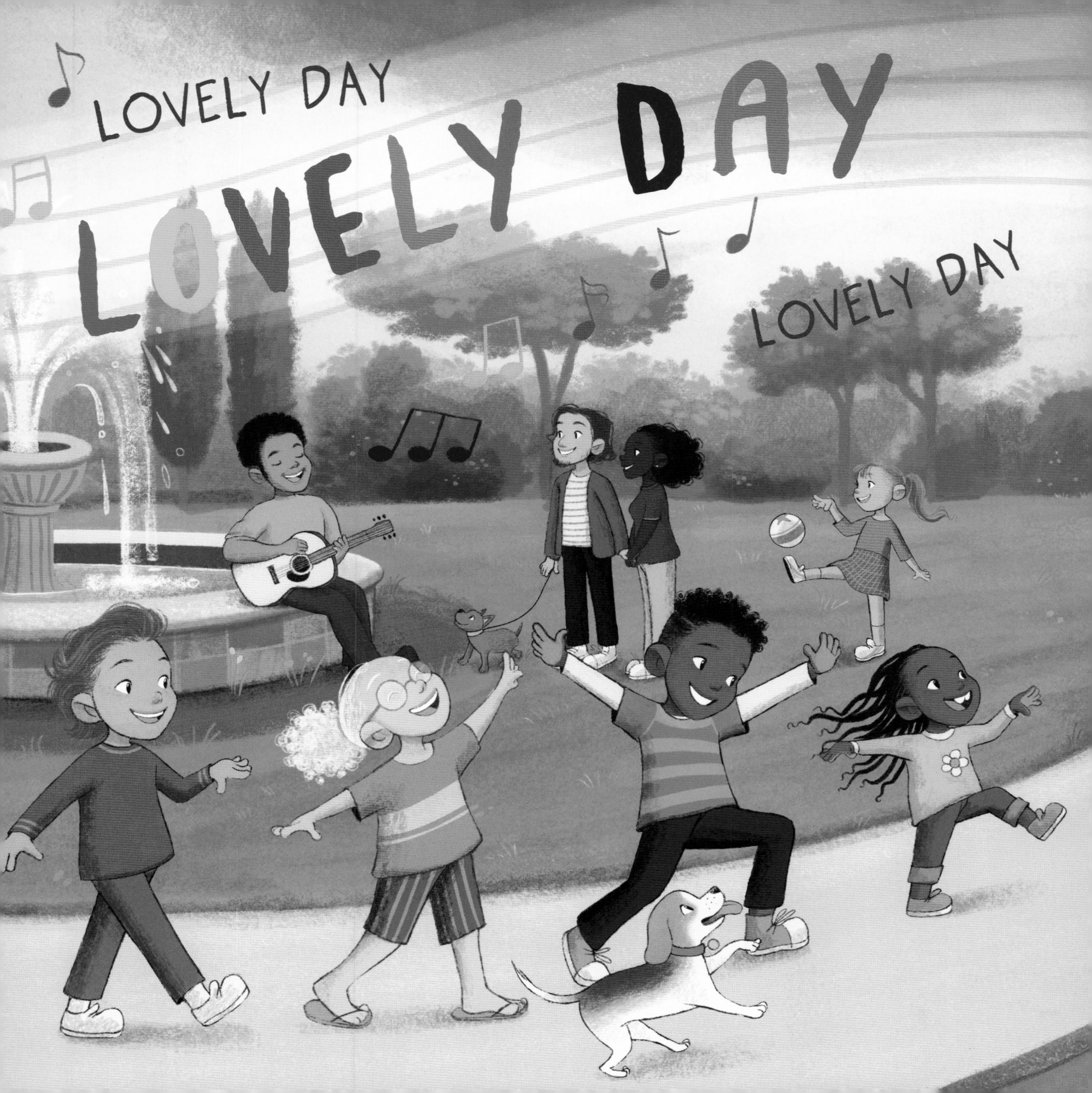
LOVELY DAY
LOVELY DAY
LOVELY DAY

When the day that lies ahead of me

Seems impossible to face . . .

And when someone else instead of me

Always seems to know the way . . .

Then I look at you

And the world's
alright with me.

Just one look at you

And I know it's gonna be . . .

A LOVELY DAY

LOVELY DAY

LOVELY DAY

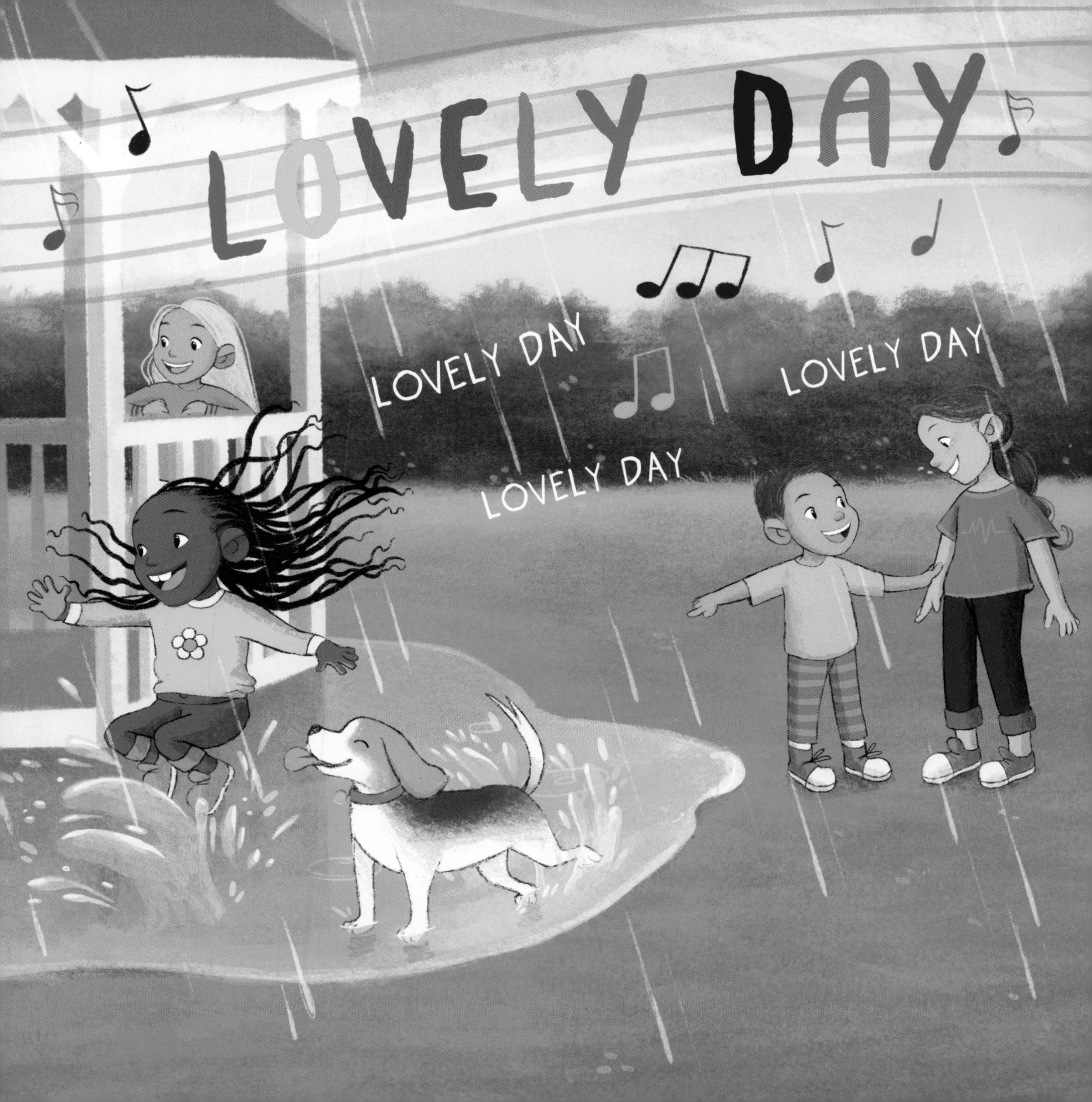
LOVELY DAY
LOVELY DAY
LOVELY DAY
LOVELY DAY